...ad... ...rent w... ...ween r... ...ers read through each level in order. You can help your young reader improve and become more confident by encouraging his or her own interests and abilities. From books your child reads with you to the first books he or she reads alone, there are I Can Read Books for every stage of reading:

SHARED READING
Basic language, word repetition, and whimsical illustrations, ideal for sharing with your emergent reader

BEGINNING READING
Short sentences, familiar words, and simple concepts for children eager to read on their own

READING WITH HELP
Engaging stories, longer sentences, and language play for developing readers

READING ALONE
Complex plots, challenging vocabulary, and high-interest topics for the independent reader

I Can Read Books have introduced children to the joy of reading since 1957. Featuring award-winning authors and illustrators and a fabulous cast of beloved characters, I Can Read Books set the standard for beginning readers.

A lifetime of discovery begins with the magical words "I Can Read!"

Visit www.icanread.com for information
on enriching your child's reading experience.

Visit www.zonderkidz.com/icanread for more faith-based
I Can Read! titles from Zonderkidz.

ZONDERKIDZ

I Can Read Fiona and the Rainy Day
Copyright © 2021 by Zondervan
Illustrations © 2021 by Zondervan

An **I Can Read Book**

Requests for information should be addressed to:
Zonderkidz, 3900 Sparks Drive SE, Grand Rapids, Michigan 49546

Softcover ISBN 978-0-310-77103-6
Hardcover ISBN 978-0-310-77104-3
Ebook ISBN 978-0-310-77105-0

Contributor: Mary Hassinger
Art direction and design: Cindy Davis

I Can Read® and I Can Read Book® are trademarks of HarperCollins Publishers.

Printed in the United States of America

21 22 23 24 25 /LSCC/ 15 14 13 12 11 10 9 8 7 6 5 4 3 2 1

ZONDER**kidz**   **1** BEGINNING READING   **I Can Read!**

Fiona and the Rainy Day

New York Times Bestselling Illustrator
Richard Cowdrey
and Donald Wu

ZONDER**kidz**

It was a cloudy day at the zoo.
It was hot too.

Fiona and Mama swam in the pool.

It had cool water.

The zookeeper came to feed Fiona
and Mama lettuce and squash.

She said, "It will storm soon, Fiona.

There will be rain.

There will be thunder and lightning."

Fiona ate lunch.

She liked rain.

She liked thunder and lightning.

They helped the trees
and flowers at the zoo grow.

Just then, Flamingo came by
Hippo Cove.
She had a pink umbrella.
"What is that?" asked Fiona.

Flamingo said, "This is an umbrella.

It is going to rain soon.

It will keep us dry when we walk."

Fiona and Flamingo saw people
with umbrellas too!
Orange and red and blue!

There was an umbrella with a smiling hippo face on it.

Two otters came down the path.
"Can we stand under your
umbrella?"
they asked Flamingo.
"Of course," Flamingo said.

Fiona, Flamingo, and the otters
watched.

The rain started falling hard.

Soon there were puddles everywhere.

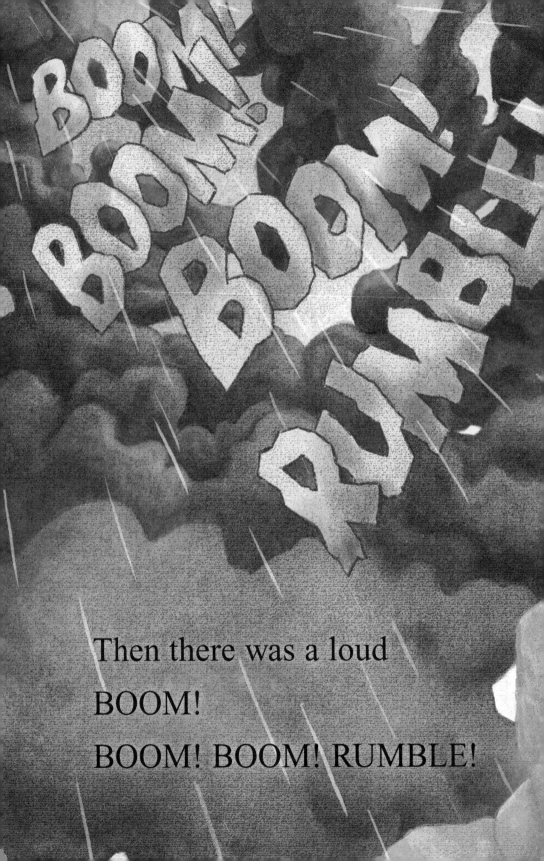

Then there was a loud

BOOM!

BOOM! BOOM! RUMBLE!

Flamingo did not like that sound.
"What is that big sound?"
she asked.

"That is thunder," said Fiona,
wiggling her ears.
"This storm will help
the trees and flowers grow.
Do not be scared!"

The animals looked at the flowers.
They were pink, white, and yellow.
Parrot was in the flowers,
hiding from the rain.

"Hello, Parrot!" Fiona called.
"Come under the umbrella with us.
We are dry."

Parrot flew over.

"Thank you! My feathers were getting all wet from the rain."

He shook out his wings.

He squawked at the thunder.

Then there was a bright flash of light.

"What was that light?"

Fiona heard a little voice.

Tortoise was hiding in his big shell.

"Come under the umbrella with us," said Fiona.

Now all the animals were under the umbrella.

"We've got this," she said and they snuggled up close.

Fiona, Flamingo, the otters,
Parrot, and Tortoise all watched.

Did their zoo friends like the storm?

Ducks quacked and played
in puddles.

Fish jumped and swam and played
like they always do.

All the monkeys went to hide
in the trees.
They went into their monkey house
to stay dry too.

Soon the rain stopped.

Flamingo put her umbrella away.

She had to go home.

Otters and Parrot waved

goodbye too.

Tortoise slowly went under a bush.

And Fiona went to swim with Mama.

Fiona liked the storm.

She liked the rain and thunder and lightning.

And Fiona loved the flowers and trees that grew because of the rain!